THE
INDIAN
SCHOOL

THE
INDIAN
SCHOOL

GLORIA WHELAN

ILLUSTRATED BY
GABRIELA DELLOSSO

SCHOLASTIC INC.
New York Toronto London Auckland Sydney

Typography by Christine Kettner

ISBN 0-590-30530-1

12 11 10 9 8 7 6 5 4   0 1 2/0

Printed in the U.S.A.   40
First Scholastic printing, October 1997

For Stephanie Spinner

ONE

It was September before they knew what to do with me. I was to go to my aunt Emma and uncle Edward. It came about in this way. A letter was sent telling them of the terrible wagon accident that killed Mama and Papa. They wrote at once kindly offering to care for me.

Uncle Edward, who was my father's brother, was a minister. Some years ago he and Aunt Emma traveled north to start a mission school for Indian children.

Just as they would take me in and care for me, so they took in and cared for the children of the Indians. Mama and Papa always spoke kindly of Uncle Edward. "He means well," Mama had said, "but he has a weakness. Just when something must be done, he cannot make up his mind."

"Emma makes up for him," Papa had answered. "She is strong enough for the two of them."

It was Aunt Emma who wrote:

September 3, 1839
Coldriver, Michigan

My dear Lucy,
Your uncle and I were greatly sorrowed to hear of the unfortunate accident that befell your dear mother and father. The Lord has gathered them into heaven. We must not question His ways.
We have arranged for Luke Jones, a blacksmith from our school, to bring you here to us. He will be in Detroit to purchase

iron the first week in September and will
return with you.

Bring only sensible clothes. Your
mother, God rest her soul, was not a
practical woman. It may be that you
have fripperies in your wardrobe. Do not
bring them. Our life here is a simple one.
It will be best if your parents' possessions
are sold. Such money as they bring can be
given over to you to provide for your
keep. There is little money to spare here.

Since you are an only child, it is likely
that you received much coddling. You
must not look to us for the kind of atten-
tion you had from your mother and
father. The good work we do in our
school for Indian children takes all of
our time. You will be welcome here but
you will be expected to do your share.

In the Lord,
Emma Wilkins

The letter seemed a cold one. It did
nothing to ease the misery I had felt since

losing my dear mama and papa. I told myself I was fortunate to have a place to go. Still, I could not be happy, for I found little welcome in my aunt's words.

I was curious about the Indian school. Indians were often seen in Detroit. They brought furs to trade. They came to collect yearly payments given in exchange for the sale of their lands. Some had taken up residence in the city. A few attended Father Richard's university. The only Indian I knew well was Waugoosh, who worked along with Papa building ships.

When the day came to leave, Mr. Jones appeared at our door. Although he was dressed as a white man, I could see he was an Indian gentleman. One of his pant legs was rolled up to reveal a wooden leg. He did not seem bothered by his infirmity but had a pleasant way about him. There played about his mouth a little smile as though his thoughts took him only to agreeable places. Though he limped badly, his arms and shoulders were those of a strong man. It was not hard to imagine him shaping iron on his anvil.

I had heeded my aunt's words, so I had only one small trunk to take with me. This Mr. Jones placed in the wagon on top of his new store of iron rods. I kept beside me a small package of books. My mama and papa had often read to me from them. When I held them, I could still hear their voices.

I bid good-bye to our elderly neighbors, Mr. and Mrs. Bontee, who had cared for me since the accident. After reading my aunt's letter, Mrs. Bontee had shaken her head. "I only wish, Lucy, that Mr. Bontee and I could keep you with us. Sadly, we are too old. You are only eleven and must have someone younger to care for you." They embraced me warmly. Mrs. Bontee had prepared a large basket of food for my journey. I wished I did not have to eat it. I wanted to keep it with me as a reminder of the Bontees' kindness.

As the wagon headed away from Detroit, I looked over my shoulder at the

town that had been my home. How often Mama and I had visited the town market. This time of year the stands were heaped with apples and plums and the pears for which our French farmers are so famous. I thought of the times Papa and I had walked down to the wharves. We loved to see the great puffing steamships and the schooners with their sails out like soaring gulls. Papa would point with great pride to those ships he had helped to build.

Mr. Jones watched me, the little smile still on his lips. "I could not live in such a town," he said. "Too many people. In the forest I pick up wood for my forge. Underneath are ants. Many, many. They run this way. They run that way. That is a town."

In no time the road took us into the woods. At first there were cabins scattered among the trees. Then there were no cabins. Only great empty fields where stumps of trees appeared to grow like some ghostly crop. "What has happened to all the trees?" I asked.

It was the only time that day the little smile left Mr. Jones' face. He took one of his hands from the reins and made a chopping motion. "That is another reason I do not like your town. All the houses there once grew in this forest."

We left the empty fields behind and entered into a wood so thick and dark the sun could not find its way into it. "How do you know where to go?" I asked. "The trails all look the same to me."

"I read the woods like you read those." He pointed to my package of books. "Look there. See the pine that stretches up higher than the others. And there, the hemlock where the lightning has bitten into it. Soon we will come to the tree where the eagle builds its nest. Tomorrow we go side by side with a stream. This land once belonged to my people, the Potawatami. In the days before I was a blacksmith, I often took this trail."

"How did you come to the Indian school?" I asked.

"When I was a young man I was about to kill a *makwa*, a bear. The bear did not like it. I did kill the bear, but first he tried to have my leg for his dinner."

I shuddered. "Are there bears where we are going?"

"Only a few," Mr. Jones said. "If you do not try to kill them, they will not try to eat you."

I resolved then and there never to kill a bear.

"After I lost my leg, I was no use to my tribe. I was no longer a good hunter. The blacksmith at your uncle's school was growing old. Your uncle told him, 'Teach Red Fox your work.' Before the school, Red Fox was my name. Now I teach Indian boys how to make a living in that little part of the world that is left to them."

The forest was filling with darkness. I worried that we would have to spend the night in the wagon. Perhaps there would be a bear in the woods. Perhaps it would know that Mr. Jones had once killed a bear. Perhaps it would be angry. "Will we have to sleep in the woods?" I asked.

"No, no. Look there. You see smoke?"

It took me a while. Finally, in the distance, I could see a wisp of white smoke curling into the darkening sky.

"It is the cabin of Mother Sally. She will take us in."

The sliver of a cabin was hidden among the trees. I could barely make it out until we were upon it. In the darkness the light from the window was a welcome sight. An old woman opened the cabin door. She had a gun pointed at us.

"Who is that? Come into the light so I can make you out."

I was too frightened to move, but Mr. Jones limped boldly up to the woman. "It's me, Mother Sally. I brought a young lady with me."

"Luke. Come in. You too, my dear." I was much relieved to see the gun laid smartly aside.

The cabin was tiny but tidy. The chairs and table looked more like trees growing out of the floor than furniture. Mother Sally was as tiny and tidy as her cabin. Her face was like a withered apple. A long gray braid tied with a shoelace hung down her back. "You are just in time," she said. "I shot some grouse this morning and they are turning on the spit."

The grouse were excellent and with them we had roasted potatoes and cider. Soon afterward we lay down to sleep. Mr. Jones rolled himself up in a blanket. Although I protested, Mother Sally gave me her cot while she curled up in a chair. Remembering the bears, I did not think I would close my eyes. Perhaps it was the warmth of the fire or the heavy meal, but I fell asleep at once.

Over our morning porridge Mother Sally said, "There is good news. My husband, Alfred, will be returning any day now. It is said he was seen on the road up from Ohio. I must take my gun and go looking for a deer. Alfred was ever fond of venison."

After many heartfelt thanks we drove off in the wagon. "Mother Sally must be very happy that her husband is returning," I said.

Mr. Jones shook his head. "She has been saying that for forty years. And still he does not come."

"Then where is he?"

Mr. Jones' small smile widened. "As far away from that gun as he can get."

In the early evening I noticed a livening in the horses. We began to follow a stream. After a bit we came upon a dozen cabins, one next to the other. With deep woods all around them, I did not wonder that they huddled together. Nearby I saw a store and a mill perched on the bank of a river. "The town of Coldriver," Mr. Jones announced. "We are only a few miles from the school." He turned to me. "I don't say anything against the school. Your uncle has been good to me." He was silent for a moment.

"You must do as your aunt says. She is a woman who likes to have her way."

I had time for no more than a hasty glance at the school grounds. There were outbuildings and fields. All was enclosed with a fence. Beyond the fence as far as you could see was the forest. The forest appeared stronger than the fence. We pulled up to a large cabin that looked to have many rooms. At once a door swung open and a man came to meet us. He was as thin as the edge of a knife, a man who would have to hang on to a tree in a windstorm if he was not to be blown away. The greater part of his lean face was hidden by whiskers the color of a ginger cat. He made one or two steps toward us and then one or two steps back. He appeared uncertain of how best to greet us.

A moment later he was pushed aside by a stout woman in a black dress. Her hair was skinned back so tightly, the corners of her eyes were slanted with the pull. She came briskly out of the cabin. "You are

Lucy. You are very welcome. I am your aunt Emma." She turned to Mr. Jones. "You may see to the horses, Luke. You are very late for dinner but there will be something for you in the kitchen." The thin man appeared to be waiting for orders. "Edward," she said to him, "don't just stand there, get the child's trunk."

As she drew me inside, she looked at the books I carried. "What have you there? Books. I must see what they are. Young minds must be kept fresh and clean."

"They are my mama and papa's books, Aunt. They often read to me from them."

She glanced at the titles. "*Ivanhoe*. That is romantic nonsense. And what is this? *The Book of English Verse*? We will find you something more sensible than poetry to read." She laid the books aside. "You have been traveling for two days and will be tired and hungry. First you must have something to eat. Then I will show you to your room. We go to bed early here and get up early."

By now Uncle Edward had returned. He reached out once or twice and finally put a gentle hand on my shoulder. "We are very pleased to have you, my dear. Your mama and papa's deaths were a great sadness to us."

"That is in the past, Edward," Aunt Emma said. "Lucy must make a new beginning."

A meager fire burned in the school's sitting room. By its light I could see several straight wooden chairs and a table with benches on either side. There were no cushions or pretty rugs and curtains, as there had been in our home in Detroit. Aunt Emma bid me sit down at the table, and called out, "Mary, bring in Miss Lucy's dinner at once."

Immediately an Indian girl of fifteen or sixteen hurried into the room with a full plate and a cup of tea. She moved silently, making no more of a stir than a shadow. Her black hair was plaited and wrapped around her head like a crown. Her eyes, which ever looked downward, had a fringe of long lashes. After placing the food in front of me, she hurried out of the room, dropping a sort of curtsy to Aunt Emma on her way.

Uncle Edward sat across from me. Aunt Emma stood over me as though impatient for me to finish. The food was tasty. There was some kind of fish along with corn and squash. I ate it gratefully, only wishing my aunt would sit down.

"It is not our custom to serve food at all hours of the day and night," Aunt Emma said. "Tonight we make an exception. After this, dinner is at five."

Uncle Edward explained, "The children from the school help out in the kitchen and need to have a good night's sleep."

When I finished, Aunt Emma called again into the kitchen and Mary quickly appeared. "You may take the dishes away, Mary, and see to the smudge on your apron. You must have gotten too close to the fire."

"Yes, ma'am," Mary said. She kept her chin tilted down but glanced quickly at me out of the corners of her large brown eyes before hastily disappearing into the kitchen.

"Tomorrow, Lucy," Aunt Emma said, "I will show you your duties. We will also begin your lessons."

Uncle Edward cleared his throat a few times. "Surely Lucy can have a day or two to become used to us, Emma?"

"It is never too soon to make a beginning, Edward. Now, Lucy, I will take you to your room."

We climbed a stairway so narrow, Aunt Emma had to gather in her skirts. In my room was all I needed but nothing else. "We have a simple life here, Lucy. The Indian children pay nothing for their keep but corn and sometimes venison. The missions can send little in the way of money. It is only by hard work and sacrifice that we manage."

My aunt left me with a caution to go to

bed at once so I would be rested for the morning. I hung my clothes upon the pegs and placed my comb and brush upon my washstand. I hoped the presence of my few belongings would make the room more familiar. But the strangeness would not go away. That night I slept fitfully, disturbed by the hooting of an owl and the cry of some animal that sounded as lonely as I.

TWO

The knock on my door came early. I
dressed at once, with only a quick glance in
the bit of mirror that hung over the washstand. The glass was so small, I was sure it
was meant for neatness and not primping.
I had seen my aunt look disapprovingly at
my wayward curls. Now I tried to pull
them into a prim straightness. Even my
freckles seemed too much decoration.

Meals were taken with the Indian students. As I entered the dining hall, all eyes

turned to me. Though the students ranged in age from infants to nearly grown-up, they were dressed alike. The boys wore corduroy trousers and cotton shirts. The girls were in calico shifts and homespun aprons. In Detroit I had been used to seeing Indians in clothes embroidered with colored beads and wearing necklaces and bracelets of beads or silver. I thought of the yellow birds that lose their bright plumage in the winter. These students all seemed to be winter birds.

As soon as breakfast was over, Aunt Emma said, "Edward, I have much to do. It would be best if you showed Lucy the school. When you return, I will quiz her to see what class she will enter."

I was glad to follow Uncle Edward outside. My aunt's busyness made no room for me.

My uncle paused, uncertain. "Shall we see the barn first or the schoolrooms? The barn, perhaps. No. Let us start with the school. We have fifteen boys and twelve girls. The Indian children come to us for many reasons. Some are brought here because they have no parents. Some come because their parents wish them to learn. They see the writing on the wall. The Indian lands are overtaken by white settlers. As the woods disappear, the animals disappear. The Indians can no longer make a living in the fur trade. The settlers do not leave the Indians enough farmland for their crops. The old life of the tribes will soon be a thing of the past. The Indians must become farmers and smiths and carpenters."

I thought it a pity that so much of the change must come from the Indians and so little from the white man.

"It is our hope," Uncle Edward went on, "that some of our students will go on to our church's academy in New York or to some other university."

We entered a room in which two older Indian girls were working at a loom while another was spinning. "This is the weaving room," Uncle Edward said. "Last year

nearly a hundred yards of cloth were woven here. The Indians seem to have a special talent for making things with their hands. At first they wished to use their own designs, and very pretty some of them were. Your aunt thought it best that the cloth be woven in a more plain design."

We went from the carpentry shop to the smithy, where Mr. Jones oversaw the work of two Indian boys. We saw the chicken coop and the cow barn. In the pasture three milk cows nosed aside fallen leaves to pull at the browning grass.

As he showed me about the school, Uncle Edward became less uncertain in manner. Proudly he pointed out where corn and potatoes had grown and where the winter wheat was planted. Rows of pumpkins and squash lay ripe and orange on the brown earth.

"Someday," he said, "we will have our own grist mill. Then we need look to no man for help." He sighed. "Now it is time to return to your aunt."

We visited the classroom where my aunt was teaching reading and writing to the younger children. When I remarked on how alike the children were dressed, Uncle Edward explained their clothes were sent from the mission.

Aunt Emma dismissed her class. She spoke to Uncle Edward as though he were one of her students. "You have been dawdling, Edward. Come now, Lucy. Let us see what you know of schoolwork."

I tried very hard.

"Well, Lucy. You are better at your reading and your sums than I would have thought. You will take your lessons with the older girls."

My aunt did not give praise easily. She closed the books and stood up. "I am sure you know less of practical things." I was led out to the henhouse and taught how to scatter the feed so all the chickens might have their share. At lunch I was told to watch over the youngest scholars and see that, like the chickens, they all shared equally.

With their dark hair, brown eyes, and golden skin they were pretty children. I could not keep from kissing the cheek of one little boy. This did not please my aunt. She warned, "If you are softhearted, the children will have no respect for you."

After that I was more prudent in my attentions. Still, a small hand would creep into mine or a tender smile reward another portion of pudding. Then my heart would soften in spite of my efforts. I tried to hide my weakness from my aunt, for I liked being among the children. I could not forget that like myself many were without father and mother.

That evening I was pleased when Aunt allowed me to help in getting the youngest boys ready for bed. Their sleeping room held narrow cots. At the foot of each cot was a small trunk for each child's clothes. The children had to be coaxed to wash their faces, for the water in the pitchers was cold. After the washing and the putting on of nightclothes, each child knelt

by his bed and said his prayers. Then my
heart became soft indeed. It was very bad
of me, but after I turned down the lamp, I
hastily kissed each child good night.

Uncle Edward said it was his custom to
read a verse or two of scripture before bed.
We settled down next to the fire. Just then
we heard a knock at the door. Uncle
Edward put down his Bible and went to
see who was there. It was an Indian man.
By his side was a small boy and a girl a year
or two older than myself. "Come in," my
uncle said. "How can we help you?"

The man took a few steps into the
room. He was dressed in a torn shirt and
soiled leggings. Though young, he was
stooped, as though he were carrying a
heavy burden. There was a frown between
his eyes and a tightness to his mouth. He
looked like he did not want to be there.
The children hung back. The man reached
down and gave each child a gentle push
forward. "I am Lost Owl. This is my son,
Star Face, and my daughter, Raven."

I thought Raven well named. Her black hair dipped on either side of her forehead like the wings of a raven. Her eyes were black and quick and sharp like the bird's eyes. Star Face was no more than five or six. His long hair was matted and snarled. His clothes, what there were of them, were in tatters. He had eyes for one thing only: a bowl of apples on the table beside him. The temptation was too much. He picked up one of the apples and began to eat it greedily.

Aunt Emma stood up. "Young man, put that down at once." The boy dropped the apple onto the table. He hid behind his father's leg, holding on for dear life. At this the girl, Raven, walked slowly over to the table. She picked up the half-eaten apple and handed it to her brother, who began to eat it again.

For a whole minute Aunt Emma was speechless. "Put that down, I say." She snatched the apple from the boy's hand. But by now she held nothing but a stem and a few seeds. She turned to Lost Owl. "Your daughter is a wicked girl. Take your children and leave here."

Uncle Edward had been taken aback by the girl's actions, but now he said, "My dear, we cannot send this man away without finding out why he has come."

"I am sorry that my children should give you trouble," Lost Owl said. "They are hungry. We have come a long way from our village. There are as many dead from smallpox as there are alive. The sickness came like a hungry fox to a nest of young birds. My wife is dead. My brother and all his family are dead. The rest of my family have gone far away so the sickness cannot find them. I was told Indian children are welcome here."

"I am not sure we have a place for children who are so lacking in manners." Though my aunt's words were hard, I saw that she was moved by Lost Owl's story.

"We have never turned away someone in need," Uncle Edward said. "Even with such sauciness we cannot begin now." There was no indecision in his voice.

Lost Owl had something more to say. "I am not giving you my children. I will go far north of here where there are still many animals. When the winter is over, I will come back with pelts. I will buy my children back."

Aunt Emma was truly shocked. "We do not buy and sell children here! What we do, we do for charity. No money will change hands. You may have your children back whenever you wish. I dare say we will be glad to be rid of them. I will promise you, though, that when they are returned you will find them much improved."

"I thank you," Lost Owl said. He bent to embrace his son. Star Face clung to him sobbing. Uncle Edward pulled him gently away. Lost Owl put his hand on Raven's shoulder in farewell. Raven stood very stiffly. She said nothing and gave no sign of sadness at her father's departure.

After Lost Owl left, I was asked to put

Star Face to bed with the younger children. At this Raven looked startled. I saw that she did not want to be parted from her brother. Still, she would not give my aunt the satisfaction of showing her distress. When Aunt Emma led her away, Raven followed along with her chin high in the air. Only once, when my aunt's attention was otherwise engaged, did Raven look quickly back at her brother. There was much love in her look. When she caught me watching, her face became stormy and closed. Timidly I asked my aunt, "May I take Star Face to the kitchen and give him some milk before I put him to bed?"

"Yes, Lucy. I should have thought of that myself. But do not call him by that foolish name. We will find a proper name for him tomorrow. Girl, would you like something as well?"

Raven shook her head. Yet she looked so thin, I was sure it was her pride and not her appetite that answered for her.

When I had warmed some milk for Star Face and fed him bread and jam, the unhappiness seemed to go out of him. He followed me like a lamb follows its mother to the small boys' dormitory. It was only when I tried to put a nightshirt on him that he rebelled. I had to let him climb into his cot in his soiled and tattered clothes. There he made a nest of his bed, burrowing into his bedclothes and curling into a ball.

That night it was not Star Face I thought of, but Raven. At last, unable to close my eyes, I crept down the hall to the girls' sleeping room. I peered in. By the light of the moon I saw Raven. She had pulled her blanket from her cot. Wrapping herself in it, she had lain down on the floor. Her shoulders were shaking with silent sobs. At first I thought of comforting her. Yet I was sure she would not like to be seen crying. I crept back to my room.

I slept no more that night. When I had first come to the Indian school, I had been brave. Seeing Raven's unhappiness, I thought of the absence of my own parents and I cried with her.

THREE

In the morning there was a terrible commotion. Aunt Emma had set to work to bathe Star Face and cut his hair. I was helping her. His howls brought Raven. She snatched the child from us and, clasping him against her, shouted, "You should not have cut his hair. Men in our tribe don't cut their hair."

"Nonsense," my aunt said. "Matthew"— for that was the name she had given Star Face—"looks much better. I will see to you when I am finished."

Raven refused to change into the school dress. "I cannot tell who I am if I look like everyone else," she insisted.

Aunt Emma warned Raven, "Do as you are told or you will not be allowed to see Matthew. I will not have him set a bad example by your behavior." After that, Raven put on the school dress.

What she refused to do was answer to her new name. My aunt had decided to call her Eleanor. Even I could see the name was not suitable. Raven fit her perfectly. As often as I heard her new name, always I thought of her as Raven. At last even my aunt was worn down. She could not get Raven's attention by using her new name. She would not call her by her given name. So she called her "girl." To that Raven would respond, but sullenly. After a few days Matthew and Raven became a part of the school.

My days were much the same. I rose early. After morning prayers I ate a quick breakfast, taken, as all of our meals were, with the Indian students. I then went to the classroom for lessons. After lunch I turned to my tasks, tending the chickens and helping Mary with dinner. Mary and I became friends. I learned from my uncle that Mary had come to Michigan from Illinois. Her family had belonged to the tribe of Chief Black Hawk. Her father, her mother, and all her sisters and brothers had perished in the battle of Bad Ax River. Any loud noise or angry word frightened her. Even my aunt noticed this. She spoke more softly to Mary than to the other students.

Once I asked Mary what her Indian name had been. Her head drooped like a wilted flower upon a stalk. She would not look at or talk with me. After that I asked no more questions. Mary was usually quiet and guarded. Sometimes, though, she liked a jest. She would hand me an empty plate for my aunt, whispering, "Your aunt needs no food. She is already as fat as a bear ready to sleep through the winter." She knew each of the little children's favorite treats. One child would get an extra piece of gingercake, another a double portion of rhubarb jam.

I helped Mary clear away the dinner dishes and put the little boys to bed. There were evening prayers, and then I, too, went to bed.

As I went about my tasks, I marveled at Uncle Edward's work with the Indians. It was only with my aunt that he was undecided. On his own he was everywhere at once. He supervised the milking of the cows. He instructed the older boys in the classroom and in the carpentry shop. He had even taught himself to speak a little of the Indian language. Some of the children, when they first came to the school, knew only a few words of English. My aunt waited for them to learn. My uncle met them on the path.

Uncle Edward made a great friend of Matthew, who followed him about and called him "Papa," much to my aunt's disapproval. Where my aunt scolded, my uncle encouraged. I thought his results were better. The students minded my uncle out of love, my aunt out of fear.

In teaching our history lessons my aunt put all the blame for the wars between the white man and the Indians upon the Indians. The children did not argue with her, but Mary looked down at her desk and caught her lip between her teeth. Only Raven spoke up. She said, "In your Bible it says if you take what does not belong to you, you will receive punishment. The white man took land that belonged to the Indians."

"It is very rude of you to contradict me, girl," my aunt snapped. "In this very country, the Iroquois Indians took land from the Sauk Indians. What do you say to that?"

Thinking of Mary, I could not be quiet. After class I said to my aunt, "There is truth in what Raven says. All of Mary's family were killed trying to protect their homes and land."

My aunt shook her head. "You are only a child. What can you understand of such things?"

I said nothing more, yet I did not like myself for giving in so easily. I marveled at Raven's courage. I did not think I would ever be brave enough to rise up against my aunt as Raven did.

Raven missed no opportunity to defy Aunt Emma. She disliked the bread served with the meals. It was a rule that the children must eat all that was served to them. I saw Raven hide bread in her pocket. Because she did not like the aprons all the girls had to wear, she smudged and soiled hers. She would purposely pretend she had not prepared her lessons. My aunt would scold her. Afterward Raven would be quick to answer the questions so that we saw she had prepared after all.

Aunt Emma punished Raven's defiance by giving her the hardest tasks. She had to scrub the floors and pare the potatoes. She did it all with an angry scowl.

I was surprised, then, when Raven went to Aunt Emma and offered to gather wild nuts. My aunt was pleased, for there was never enough money for all the school needed. A supply of nuts for breads and sweets would be welcome. I was sent along with Raven. "You will see where these trees are, Lucy, so that you can find them when the girl is no longer with us." Raven did not seem pleased at my company but said nothing.

It was October now. In the sunlight the maples looked as if they had been hung with hundreds of scarlet lanterns. The birches, like Uncle Edward, could not make up their minds. Half were green and half gold. Watching over everything were pines so tall you could not see to the top of them without bending back your head. Winding through the woods was a narrow branch of the Coldriver. Leaning over the stream were willow trees, the tresses of their branches waving in the light wind.

All afternoon I followed Raven about as we filled our baskets. I was amazed at what she found: butternuts, hickory nuts, hazel-nuts, and walnuts. Each kind of tree had its own place in the woods. The walnut trees were often along the bank of the stream. "The nuts fall into the water," Raven said. "The stream carries them along for many miles. Then they find a home on the shore and become trees."

These were the first words Raven had spoken to me.

"Did you have to do as much work in your village as you do here?" I asked.

"More. I gathered wood. I fished, putting out nets and gathering them in. I planted the corn and harvested it. I helped with the maple syrup. That is what I liked best."

I had never heard Raven have so much to say. Hoping to encourage her, I sat down. After a moment she settled next to me. "Why did you like it best?" I asked.

"In the spring, when we have warm days and cold nights, the men return from their hunting. Many trees are tapped. The syrup drips into birch-bark pails. The pails are gathered and emptied into great kettles. All night long the kettles boil over the campfire. We have songs and dances for the sugaring. You have many maples here. I wonder you do not make syrup."

"Perhaps my aunt and uncle do not know how. Could you teach them?"

"I think no one could teach your aunt."

I ought to have disagreed, but I could not.

As we went deeper and deeper into the woods, Raven seemed a different person. The sullen scowl left her face. She watched a trout fanning its tail in the stream's clear water. She smiled at the clumsy grouse that flew up with a great racket as we approached. She showed me many things: a mud chute on the bank of the stream where otters slid, a hump of rushes that was a muskrat's home, a poplar limb with tooth marks from a beaver. The forest had become my classroom.

We were just about to turn back with our full baskets when Raven saw the tree.

It was a great oak. A long while before, lightning must have opened a gash in the trunk. Over the years the tree had rotted and the opening had widened to a huge hollow. Raven and I both were able to squeeze inside. There were droppings and bones in and about the tree. Raven named the animals that had once lived there: a porcupine, a groundhog, a skunk, and even a bear. At that I recalled Mr. Jones' story and looked hastily about.

As we turned back toward the school, Raven was quiet. She no longer paid attention to my questions. She was thinking of something, but she would not tell me what it was.

FOUR

Each day Raven would ask if she might go into the woods. When enough nuts had been gathered, she offered to pick up kindling and pinecones for the fire. My aunt grew suspicious. I heard her tell my uncle, "She will revert to the way of her pagan people and forget all we have taught her here at the school."

"I believe Raven just likes being out-of-doors," Uncle said. "It is what she is used to."

My aunt put an end to Raven's trips into the woods. Once again Raven grew silent and angry. Her black eyes were fierce when she looked at Aunt Emma. One fine afternoon when Raven had been set to scraping carrots for our dinner she slipped out of the kitchen. Against my aunt's wishes she went into the woods. When she returned, my aunt was waiting for her. "You have been disobedient. I told you when you first came that if you did not follow the rules of the school, you would not be able to spend time with your brother. I will not have you set Matthew a bad example."

This was hard on Raven, for she looked forward to the time after dinner each evening when she was allowed to be with Matthew. Often she had saved secretly for him some tasty morsel from her own dinner. Or she had some little toy to amuse him. Once it was a handful of pretty stones she had gathered from the river bottom. Another time she made a bird with the dried pod of a milkweed for wings.

I believe it was more than Raven's dis-
obedience that made my aunt keep Raven
from spending time with Matthew. A
rivalry had grown up between Raven and
Aunt Emma for Matthew's affections.
Matthew was clever at his lessons. He was
a loving child who easily attached himself
to anyone who paid him attention. He followed my uncle about. He was just as
loving to me as I put him into bed at night.
Even my aunt Emma, who made no
friends among the students, allowed
Matthew to climb upon her lap. He would
catch on to her apron strings and follow her
about. Aunt Emma could not even bring
herself to scold Matthew for any little mis-
chief he made.

Matthew had not noticed that Aunt
Emma would frown when he put his arms
around Raven. He had not noticed Raven's
scowl when he climbed onto Aunt Emma's
lap. He was a child who trusted everyone.

Now that Raven was forbidden to spend
time with Matthew, Aunt Emma had him

for herself. This, along with many loud scoldings from my aunt, was more than Raven could bear. One morning Raven was gone, leaving behind a note.

I will not stay in this prison. I go north to my father.

Aunt Emma was furious. Uncle Edward was worried. "We have promised their father to care for his children. This is very bad." After many false starts he hitched up the wagon. He set out on the road north to look for Raven, but by the day's end he was back. "There is no sign of her. No one has seen her. Most likely she has kept to the woods rather than travel the road. I have urged that word be sent to us if she is discovered."

"She is an insolent child," my aunt said. "I believe Matthew will do better apart from her and her stubborn ways."

Matthew did not do better. When he missed his sister at supper, he asked where she was. When she was not there at break-fast, he cried. It was not until the third day that he regained his sweet temper. Aunt Emma said, "He has forgotten her, and just as well."

Matthew had not forgotten Raven. As I put him to bed that night, I plumped his pillow. Underneath the pillow was a tiny animal, a porcupine, fashioned of a pine-cone and pine needles. I knew Matthew had not had it before. No matter how I coaxed him, he would not tell me where it

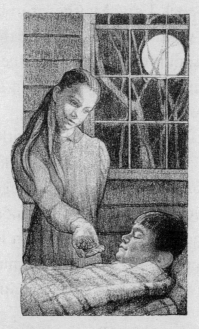

had come from. I put it back under his pillow and said nothing. I knew where it had come from. Raven had brought it to him while he was outdoors playing. She was somewhere near. That was why Matthew was happy once again.

The next afternoon I offered to look after the small boys while they played outside. I watched for Raven but she did not come. For several more days I watched. The beginning of the following week, when the children were playing a game of hide-and-seek I saw Matthew run into the woods. It was a long while before the other children could find his hiding place. When he was finally discovered, he had a fistful of hickory nuts.

Later, finding my aunt busy with a stew she was cooking for dinner, I asked if I might take a little walk. "Run along," Aunt Emma said. "You are only underfoot here."

I did not know where to begin looking. I wandered through the part of the woods where Raven and I had collected nuts. The trees were bare. Their black branches were silhouetted against a gray sky. The Indian children spoke of October as the month of the falling leaf. Now it was November, the freezing month. That morning when I had gone out to get water I had to crack the ice on the rain barrel. I pulled my shawl around me and wished I had taken my mittens. If Raven was here in the woods, she would have to have a shelter at night. It was then that I thought of the lightning tree.

At first I could not find it. One tree looked much like another to me. When I came to the stream, I recalled how Raven and I had followed it looking for walnut trees. Now its edges were embroidered with ice. I hurried along beside it until I came to the tree. There was no one there, but smoke from a damped fire scrawled upward like a secret message.

"Raven," I called. "Raven, I know you're there. I promise not to tell." I waited. "Please, Raven. I need to see you."

After a moment Raven appeared. She

looked more like a wood sprite than a student at the Indian school. Her dress was torn and her hair a tangle. "You said you were going north," I said.

"I could not leave my brother. I said that so no one would look here for me."

"What do you have to eat?"

Raven led me to the tree. Inside were birch-bark baskets of dried fruit and nuts. "The cranberries are ripe in the bog near here. Yesterday I caught a turtle."

"A turtle! How could you cook it?"

"I roasted it in its shell."

I shuddered. "But you'll freeze to death when winter comes."

"I don't care. I will never go back to your aunt. There are ducks who feed upon fish and you cannot eat them for their bad taste. They are good for nothing. That is your aunt."

I did not think my aunt would be happy to be compared to a duck. "She is not so cross as she seems," I said. "She is very fond of Matthew."

"My brother does as she tells him. He runs after her like a baby goose following its mother."

Now Aunt Emma was not only a duck but a goose.

"I am not a little goose," Raven said. "I will not follow her."

As we spoke, there was a whirring sound and the sky darkened. Overhead a great flock of passenger pigeons turned the sky into a feathered river. They were on their way south. Some of the birds sifted down onto nearby trees. They rested on the branches, unafraid of us. Raven picked up a heavy log. She swung at the birds. A moment later three of them lay dead at our feet.

Quickly Raven began to pluck one of the birds. I took another in my hands. It was still warm. The bird was bluish-gray with a breast the color of a fiery sunset. I was shocked at how eagerly Raven had killed it. Still, in all my life I had never had to go without food. I knew that if I were hungry, I, too, would have killed the birds.

I handed the small, limp body to Raven. "I must go or my aunt will be suspicious."

"You won't give me away?"

I promised I would not. "Is there anything I can bring you?"

"A fishhook and some string."

When I returned to the school, I kept my promise not to betray Raven. Yet it was hard for me to look my aunt and uncle in the eye. When my uncle read from the scripture that evening, it seemed the psalm was meant for me: "He that worketh deceit shall not dwell within my house: he that telleth lies shall not tarry in my sight." After that I was glad to creep up to my bed and hide.

FIVE

All the rest of the week I stayed away from Raven. I had some idea that if I did not see her, I was not deceiving my aunt and uncle. Still, Raven was always on my mind. The sun was weaker, the days shorter, the nights colder. When I saw no new toy in Matthew's hands, I began to worry. I waited until Sunday was over, thinking it a double sin to deceive my aunt and uncle on the Sabbath. Monday afternoon I took a fishhook from my uncle's cupboard and some string from my aunt's ball of twine. I stuffed my pockets with apples and corn bread and went into the woods.

When I came to the lightning tree, I found Raven looking thinner. She seemed pleased to see me and eagerly ate the food I brought. Looking into the tree, I saw that the birch-bark baskets were nearly empty.

"How is Matthew?" she asked. "I see him every day, but I do not go close."

"He is fine. Raven, won't you come back to the school? The nights are so cold."

"I cannot go back now. Your aunt would be upon me like a fox on a rabbit."

"What will happen when the snows come?"

"There is a story of an Indian girl who was lost in a snowstorm and never found. After the storm her tribe looked up into the sky. They saw stars in the shape of a snowflake. They knew then what had happened to her. Perhaps that is what will happen to me."

I did not want Raven to turn into a bunch of stars. I wanted her to stay on earth and be my friend.

Raven began turning over logs until she found a pale crawly thing with many wriggling legs. She stuck it on the fishhook I had brought. Tying the string onto a branch, she cast the twitching bug out over the water. Again and again Raven sent the bug out. Suddenly a trout leaped out of the water. A moment later the trout lay on the grassy bank, its tail slapping the ground. I looked away as Raven slammed its head against a rock. With a thin-edged stone she cut open the belly to clean the fish.

"There was a lake by our village," she said. "At night we would get into canoes, carrying with us birch-bark torches. The torches made the water bright so we could see the fish but they could not see us. Then the men sent spears into the fish. They were not fish like this one but *namah*, a great fish. One of those fish would feed many people. You looked out in the black night and saw over the lake the canoes with their torches. They were like great fireflies skimming over the water."

"In Detroit the fishing boats went out in the early morning," I said. "Late in the afternoon they returned. Mama and I often went down to the waterfront to meet the boats. Mama would pick out a whitefish for our supper and we would take it home with us. Raven, do you think of your mother?"

"She goes with me."

"My mother is often with me as well."

That night as I lay snug in my warm bed, I resolved next day to bring Raven a blanket.

Extra blankets for the cots were kept in a chest. In the afternoon, after I had put on my cloak, I took one of the blankets from the chest. I wrapped it around me under the cloak and hurried out of the house. I had not received permission to go into the woods, so I hastily handed the blanket to Raven and turned to go.

"I cannot take this," Raven said. "Your aunt will guess where I am."

"It's a blanket that is not used. She will never notice." I thrust the blanket back and returned quickly to the school.

I was wrong. She did notice. The next day Matthew came down with fever and chills. Aunt Emma went to get an extra blanket for him. "Mary," she called, "there are only three blankets here. Where is the other one?"

Mary looked puzzled. "I have not seen the blanket."

"Nonsense. No one else takes things from this chest. Do not lie to me."

Mary's head drooped. Tears hung like drops of dew on her long lashes. "I do not have the blanket."

"You have stolen the blanket and sold it for money."

This was very terrible to me. "I took the blanket, Aunt Emma."

Aunt Emma turned to me. "If you were cold and required another blanket, you should have said something. I do not see why you should be spoiled with two blankets when one is all that is required. Bring the blanket here."

She would have noticed had I taken the blanket from my bed. I could not say that I had taken the blanket to Raven, for I had promised not to give her away. "I d-don't have t-two blankets," I stammered.

"Then where is the other blanket? Speak up, Lucy."

When a child was sick we often held the child's blanket to the fire to warm it and keep the child cozy. "I was warming Matthew's blanket. I scorched it so badly, I hid it and took another for Matthew's bed." This was a very bad lie. I would not have been surprised if a bolt of lightning had been hurled at me from on high. I would have welcomed it. Nothing would have suited me more than disappearing in a puff of smoke. But no welcome bolt of lightning appeared.

"Where did you hide it?"

"I buried it."

"What! Buried it! You must have taken leave of your senses. Where did you bury it?"

"I don't remember. Someplace in the woods."

My aunt became very red and puffed up. "You are an ungrateful and foolish girl. This is how you repay our taking you in. With your carelessness you destroy valuable property."

I believe there would have been much more, but just then Uncle Edward hurried into the room. "Emma, you must come at once. Matthew's fever has risen. He is delirious."

At that we all hastened to Matthew's bedside. To keep the other children from catching his illness, Matthew was in a room by himself. We saw at once that his condition had grown worse. His face was flushed. He was having trouble breathing. From time to time he would cry out Raven's name. Most worrisome of all was a rash that had appeared on his face and body. We all thought the same thing. Smallpox. The illness that had killed so many of the Indians.

"I have sent Luke for a doctor," Uncle Edward said. "But it will take another day for him to get here."

My evil doings with the blanket were forgotten. Aunt Emma knelt by Matthew's bedside. It was the first time I had seen her appear helpless. She turned to Uncle Edward. "What must we do?"

Uncle Edward said, "He is crying for his sister. It is a pity Raven is not here. She would be a comfort to him."

"Can we not find her?" Aunt Emma asked. In her worry over Matthew she had forgotten all her complaints about Raven.

"How can we find her? When she ran away, we could not discover a trace of her."

Matthew called again for Raven. Aunt Emma looked up at Uncle Edward. "I drove her away with my scoldings. Now we may lose Matthew because of my hardness."

63

I could be silent no longer. "Raven is here," I said.

Uncle Edward looked at me. His voice was as stern as I have ever heard it. "Lucy, you see how sick Matthew is. You see what state your aunt is in. What foolishness can this be?"

The words I had held in for so many days came pouring out in one breath. "Raven never ran away. She didn't want to leave Matthew. She is staying nearby in the woods in a great tree with a hollow. She eats berries and nuts and roasts turtles. I gave the blanket to her so she would not freeze to death at night. I can get her at once."

I did not wait a moment. Uncle Edward and Aunt Emma stared openmouthed at me as I ran from the room.

SIX

I did not stop to throw on my cloak, but the coldness was nothing to me. I do not think my feet touched the ground. I was sure Raven would return with me. But when I blurted out my story to her, Raven shook her head.

"It is a trick to bring me back to your prison."

"Indeed, it is not. Matthew calls for you. His life may depend upon your returning to calm him."

There must have been something in the urgency of my voice that persuaded her. Within moments she was running ahead of me. When I reached the school, she was already with Matthew, cradling him in her arms. Tears ran down her cheeks. Angrily she looked at my aunt and uncle. "You promised my father to care for us."

Aunt Emma was too upset to answer. Uncle Edward said, "We would not have Matthew sick for the world. But such things happen. We have sent for a doctor. He will be here tomorrow."

With Raven there Matthew grew quieter. He fell into a fitful sleep, but his breath came in short gasps. Raven stayed with him all night, as did my aunt. I could not sleep and looked into the room from time to time. Often I would find Raven and Aunt Emma joined together in some task to make Matthew comfortable. Aunt Emma would dip a cloth into cool water and wring it out. Raven would take it and lay it gently upon Matthew's forehead. Raven would carefully lift Matthew from his bed while Aunt Emma spread a clean sheet under him. No word passed between them. Yet their hands working together was surely a kind of language.

In the morning Uncle and I begged them to get some sleep while we watched over Matthew. They would not leave him.

Raven had noticed Matthew's rash at once. She shook her head. "It is not the smallpox rash."

"I pray you are right," Uncle Edward said.

That afternoon the doctor arrived. Dr. Windsor had bright blue eyes that looked right through your skin to your very bones. At once he took over, sending Raven and Aunt Emma from the room. "You must leave it to me now," he said, and shooed them away.

We stood outside the door waiting. The moment he came out, Uncle Edward asked, "Is it smallpox, Doctor?" He worried not only for Matthew but for all the students.

Dr. Windsor shook his head. "No, indeed. It is merely chicken pox that has gone awry. It is a rare happening with chicken pox, but pneumonia has developed. That is the cause of Matthew's troubles. His fever is high. Today should tell the tale. I will remain with you. You may continue to nurse the boy. It is all we can do for him at the moment."

Raven and Aunt Emma hastened back into the room. Mary and I brought basins of water from the kitchen. Uncle Edward paced back and forth in the hallway, his lips ever moving in prayer. Matthew tossed and shook like a leaf in a high wind. He mumbled words that made no sense. From time to time the doctor silently entered the sickroom, and then left just as silently. Though we looked hard, we saw no sign of hope upon his face.

Darkness fell and a full moon, the

freezing moon, shone through the windows of Matthew's room. It frosted everything in its path. One candle burned in a far corner so as not to disturb Matthew's sleep. "Surely his breathing is more steady," Aunt Emma said to the doctor.

"You are right. The crisis is passed. I believe the boy will recover. We can all get some rest now." Raven and Aunt Emma refused to leave. When I looked into the room, I saw them asleep beside Mathew's bed, their heads resting on either side of his pillow.

In the morning Matthew was so improved that Dr. Windsor took leave of us. Uncle Edward attempted to pay him, but he would take no fee. "I have looked around at your school and I see what good work you are doing for these children. Where they might have gone hungry, here they have food. You are preparing them for some useful work so they may find a place in the world. Still, I think it is a sorry thing that they must give up their old ways."

Matthew's appetite returned. Aunt Emma found tasty morsels for him and shared his care with Raven. Because Matthew so often called his sister by her name, Aunt Emma fell into the practice also. They were not friends, but they were no longer enemies. At first Raven spoke of leaving, but Matthew cried so, she promised to stay.

I did not see how she could go back into the woods. Snow covered everything. One thing looked like another. Even if Raven curled up like a bear in the lightning tree, she would not survive. I thought of the Indian girl she had told me about. One night I would have looked up to see stars scattered into a snowflake.

Winter seemed to go on forever. Very little food was left. The portions on our plates grew smaller. Uncle Edward and Aunt Emma took almost nothing for themselves. Uncle Edward grew thinner than ever. Aunt Emma looked like an upholstered chair that had lost its stuffing.

There was little to eat besides carrots, cabbages, and turnips. The cows gave little milk and the salt pork was gone. Apart from a few rabbits shot by Luke Jones there was no meat. Mr. Jones declared that if only he could get to the cedar swamp, where the deer wintered, he would surely find meat for us. Unhappily, with his wooden leg he could walk no more than a few feet in the deep snow. Uncle Edward offered to try to get a deer. But everyone knew how helpless he was with a rifle. He held it as though it were a snake about to bite him.

Raven listened to Mr. Jones' complaints. The next day she told him, "I will make you a special snowshoe."

Aunt Emma said, "That is a foolish idea. How can Luke fit a snowshoe onto a wooden leg?"

"Often I helped my mother in the making of snowshoes," Raven said.

Mr. Jones looked at Raven with the

little smile that was ever on his face. "Let her try."

My uncle seesawed. "You may lose one of the snowshoes in the woods. How would you get back? Yet these children must have more to eat." At last he agreed.

Raven hurried into the woods, returning with branches from an ash tree. As we stood about watching, she heated the ash until she could bend it into the shape of a bear paw. She attached small branches to the frame with twine. Finally she wove more branches in and out of the bear paw. The snowshoe would be laced to Mr. Jones' good foot. Into the center of a second snowshoe she wove a small board. The wooden leg would be fastened to the board.

Mr. Jones was excited. Eagerly he wrapped himself in warm clothes. My uncle insisted on going along. "I cannot let you go into the woods in this weather by yourself."

"You must stay here," Mr. Jones told

him. "You are not a man who can go into the woods quietly. The deer will scatter like a flock of birds. I must go alone."

We all stood at the doorway to see Luke Jones off. At first he had difficulty moving over the snow. After a bit he traveled more easily. We followed him with our eyes until he was no more than a speck against the white snow.

Uncle Edward paced back and forth. Aunt Emma set Mary and Raven and myself to sweeping and cleaning. Aunt worked harder than any of us, washing away her worry in soap and scrubbing.

Hours passed. Uncle Edward was just about to set off for the cedar swamp when a cry went up from some younger boys watching at a window. There was Luke Jones moving slowly across the surface of the deep snow.

With no thought for the cold or our lack of boots we all ran out to meet him. As he drew closer he held up a haunch of meat. Though it was dripping blood, we had no pity for the unfortunate deer. As we cheered, we thought only of full plates and bellies. Uncle Edward fashioned a sleigh to bring the deer from the cedar swamp to the school. That night a portion of the deer was roasted and served up, accompanied by loud cheers for Mr. Jones. For once no one left the table hungry.

SEVEN

Early in March the snow began to draw in on itself. It pulled away from the roads. It disappeared from the south-facing hills. In the woods each tree had a circle about it bare of snow. Raven grew restless. "Soon it will be sugaring time," she said. She looked longingly at the maple trees.

The first week in March I celebrated my twelfth birthday. I said nothing about it, but Aunt Emma mentioned it at breakfast. "You will do your usual tasks," she said, "for you would not wish to begin a new year by shirking your responsibilities." I expected nothing more.

Dinner that evening began as usual. I poured the milk for the younger children and buttered their bread. As I sat down to my own meal, I was surprised to discover a number of packages at my place. There was a thimble from Aunt Emma. Uncle Edward gave me a small book of hymns. The younger children had printed out a Bible verse for me in their neatest script: THE MEEK SHALL INHERIT THE EARTH. Luke Jones had fashioned a pretty heart-shaped trivet on his forge. From Raven there was a small decorated box made of birch bark. Aunt Emma admired the box. "It is quite pretty and required no materials other than those free for the taking. A thrifty gift." It was the first time I had heard her admire something of Indian design.

It was my first birthday without my parents. Even in my pleasure at all I had been

given, I could not keep from thinking of them. In my longing to bring them closer, I turned to my aunt. "I am twelve now, Aunt Emma. Could I not have my book of poetry back?"

"You must not think you are a grown woman at twelve, Lucy. You have your schoolbook and a very pretty book of hymns from your uncle. With my thimble you can find pleasure in sewing. I do not see that you need to occupy your mind with words written to amuse rather than instruct."

When Aunt Emma got her stern look, I

thought of the chapter in the Bible where the people of Israel march into the land of Canaan. Joshua smites the Canaanites with the edge of his sword and destroys them utterly. I would have made no reply for fear of a smiting from my aunt. But I had seen Raven stand up to Aunt Emma many times and she had not been smitten and utterly destroyed.

I took a deep breath. "There is a pretty poem about spring and daffodils. May I not copy that out of the book to keep us cheerful until the real spring comes?"

"Very well, Lucy, but you must not get into the habit of coaxing."

My insistence had won me my book. I was less sure it was the meek who would inherit the earth.

All that week Raven had kept an eye on the trail that led through the woods. Whenever she had a spare moment, I found her looking northward. "Hunting time is over," she told me. "My father will surely come now."

By the end of the week Lost Owl was with us. He stood straighter. The burden he had carried seemed lifted from him. Matthew ran to him and clung to his leg as though it were the mast on some storm-tossed ship. Raven stood close beside him. She said little but her eyes were lively. I saw her hand steal into her father's.

"I went far north to country across the great lake," Lost Owl said, "to the country of the British. There are still many animals there. The winter was cold, so the pelts were thick. They brought me a good sum. Now I will take my son and daughter back to my village. Before we leave, I will do something to thank you for caring for them. I am a good hunter. I can put meat on your table."

Everyone was pleased at this, for our venison had been eaten up long ago. The story of Luke Jones' trip into the swamp was told.

Raven tugged at Lost Owl's arm. "Father, can we not show them how we take sap from the maple trees?"

Uncle Edward protested. "We cannot ask too much of Lost Owl."

Aunt Emma was not so reluctant. "Nonsense. It would give us a sweetener the year round. There would be a great saving in not having to buy sugar. If we could get enough, we might even trade or sell some of it." Aunt Emma was pleased at the idea of wringing syrup from the trees. She also saw that this would delay Matthew's departure. She could not refuse Lost Owl his son. But she was in no hurry to have her favorite taken from her.

When the sugaring commenced, the whole school was put to work. Every pail and vessel was rounded up. From the kitchen came kettles and saucepans. The horses' oat buckets were borrowed. Raven showed us how to make birch-bark pails. The students were sent into the woods to gather fallen branches for firewood. Uncle Edward and Lost Owl cut down all the dead trees they could find.

When all was ready, the trees were

tapped. As the pails filled with sap, they were gathered and brought to a great kettle. We all stood by as Mr. Jones brought a glowing coal from his forge. The kindling caught fire. Flames flared up. The kettle boiled day and night. Mr. Jones, Lost Owl, and Uncle Edward took turns feeding the fire. However late at night I looked out of my window, I saw the blaze of flames against the black night sky. Huddled next to the warmth of the fire was a lone figure keeping watch.

Some of the syrup was preserved in bottles. A very little was poured onto clean snow. It hardened like taffy and we all had it as a treat. The rest of the syrup was boiled until it thickened. It was then placed in a great pan. Like witches stirring their brew, we took turns paddling the sticky mixture until it turned into sugar. We had the sugar on our porridge and in our corn cakes. Raven said dog was very tasty cooked in maple syrup, but we did not think of trying that.

By the end of March the sugaring was completed. My uncle and aunt were grateful for all that Lost Owl had done. Uncle Edward had something to say to Lost Owl. After one or two attempts he announced, "Lost Owl, you would be most welcome to stay here at the school. You can teach the students to sow and harvest our crops. In the winter you can hunt and in the spring there will be the maple syrup. You will have a home here and Matthew and Raven can continue their schooling."

"Matthew is a bright little boy," Aunt Emma said. "He will do well in school." After a moment she added, "Raven is bright as well. She will profit by staying here and continuing to improve her deportment." My aunt spoke in her usual stern way. Yet I saw how softly she looked at Matthew. Though she would not say so, she had grown to care for Raven as well. During the making of the maple sugar she had seen how hard Raven worked and how quickly she obeyed her father.

For myself I longed to have them remain. Like my aunt I felt tender toward Matthew. What I cared about most was having Raven stay. Though there were many students at the school, if she went away I would be very much alone.

Lost Owl was silent for a moment. The frown that he had lost returned. "I thank you, but it cannot be. Our home is in our village. My sister will come there to help me care for Star Face and Raven. Though I leave, I will not forget your kindness."

When I copied out the poem about the daffodils, I found some lines that I wrote out for Raven:

> *But if the while I think on thee, dear friend,*
> *All losses are restored and sorrows end.*

When the time came for parting, I gave her the piece of paper on which I had written the bit of Shakespeare's poem. Raven took the paper but said no word to me. There was a distant look in her eyes. In her thoughts I believe she was already back in her village.

It was different with Matthew. He put his arms around me and then burrowed into the folds of Aunt Emma's apron. At first he refused to be separated from her. At last Lost Owl tempted him away with a promise that he should have his own bow and arrows. At that he went happily. I thought life would be pleasant for Matthew. Everyone loved him. If one friend passed out of his life, soon there would be another to take that friend's place.

The whole school was there to say good-bye. Afterward I stood at the door with my aunt while the three figures grew smaller and smaller. At last there was nothing to see but the empty trail. Aunt Emma put her arm around me and drew me to her. In all the months I had been

there it was the first time she had shown me such affection. I could not hold back my tears. I would miss Raven. I also envied her. I longed to have my mother and father return, as Lost Owl had returned, and take me away with them. As my aunt pressed me to her, I felt her tears mingle with mine. At last she pulled away. Straightening her skirts, she said, "I cannot stand here all day when there is work to be done. Go to the kitchen, Lucy, and see if you cannot be of help to Mary."

Like myself, Mary had been thinking of her family. I found her standing in the middle of the kitchen, her hands at her sides. "I have just remembered my Indian name," she said. "It is Wabomeme, which means 'dove.' Will you call me that when we are alone, as you called Raven by her name? Only please don't tell your aunt."

I promised that I would. "Wabomeme, would you like to go back to your tribe?"

Mary shook her head sadly. "It would be like looking for snow on a summer's day.

My tribe have all melted away. Besides, all my ways now are the ways of white people. I have forgotten how to live in the tribe."

Later that night when I was alone in my room I took up the birch-bark box that Raven had made. I was still hurt at how she had left without a look or word for me. I opened the little box to smell the sweet grass that was woven around the inside.

I thought of all Raven had taught me. She had shown me where to gather nuts in the forest and how to make maple syrup. I had seen her stand up to my aunt. Living in the lightning tree, she had shown me how you can survive on your own. Raven had been to the school for Indians, but I had been to Indian school.